Kentucky Adventures

Amy Barkman

Illustrations by Malinda A. Raines

Kentucky Adventures
© 2014, 2016 by Amy Barkman

Cover Illustration and Interior Illustrations
by Malinda A. Raines

Cover Design by Ginny Smith

ISBN: 978-0-9983520-1-5

This book is dedicated to people of all ages who love adventures. I hope these "what if's" encourage you to adventure into your own, and make all history come alive for you.

Contents

Adventure One
Archaeological Dig

When the doorbell rang early Saturday morning, Mary Beth raced down the stairs to answer it. She threw the door open to find her best friend, Christy, on the front porch.

"Are you ready?" Christy bounced on her toes as if she could not keep her excitement in check.

Mary Beth felt exactly the same. The day was finally here!

"You bet I am." Grabbing her jacket from the hall closet, she turned her head and shouted over her shoulder toward her older brother. "David, it's time to go."

In less than ten seconds she was running down the porch steps, David's feet clattering on the stairs behind her. She tumbled through the back door of Christy's father's car and took the middle seat next to Slicker, her brother's best friend, while Christy buckled her seatbelt up front beside her dad.

Slicker jerked his head toward her in a nod, excitement giving his eyes an extra sparkle. "Hey."

Mary Beth smiled in answer as David slid in beside her. She'd been looking forward to today for weeks. Her insides felt jerky, and she couldn't stop smiling. How funny was that? When she first heard that there was an archeological dig right here in Danville, she'd thought, *How boring. So what?* But then her parents arranged for them to actually volunteer at the dig site. Who would have thought a ten-year-old girl could do something as cool as digging for bones and stuff that were thousands of years old?

"I hope you've all got warm jackets,"

said Christy's father as he backed the car out of the driveway. "The sun's shining, but that wind is going to be cold today."

"We'll be okay, Dad." Christy turned in the front seat to exchange an excited grin with Mary Beth.

The drive didn't take long. The hilltop where the archeologist had set up his command tent was not very far out of town. The minute the car came to a stop, Slicker and David both opened their doors and tumbled out. Mary Beth took a bit longer to exit the car.

"Thank you for driving us, Mr. Lane," she said.

"You're welcome, Mary Beth." Mr. Lane waved in their direction. "I'll be back to pick you up at four o'clock. Have fun getting your hands dirty."

She and Christy shared a giggle as they waved goodbye and watched his car pull away. They looped arms and turned around. A nice-looking young man with a beard stood nearby holding a clipboard. He wore jeans, a tee shirt, and a jeans jacket, and peered at them through thick glasses.

"Are you Christy Lane and Mary Beth Thompson?" he asked.

They nodded. "Yes sir."

The young man looked at David and Slicker. "And you're David Thompson and Sidney Bell?"

Sidney? Mary Beth and Christy both giggled, which drew a glare from Slicker.

"That's right," answered David.

The man nodded. "Good. My name's Cliff Niquette, and I'm the archeologist."

Mary Beth exchanged a glance with Christy, who arched her eyebrows. Somehow they'd expected him to be older.

"Okay, you'll each be working with a professional member of my team."

They wouldn't be able to stay together? Mary Beth tried hard not to frown, and Christy was doing the same.

Mr. Niquette pointed toward the hillside, where there were several squares of earth dug out in the green grass. None of the squares was very deep. "We're sifting the soil through a screen a little bit at a time." A grin carved dimples in his cheeks above his beard. "Let's keep our fingers crossed that you'll find some interesting stuff."

Mary Beth gave Christy's hand a final squeeze and then filed after a young woman with her hair in a ponytail. She paid close attention to the instructions she was given. Her job was to break up little clumps of dirt that were shoveled into a screen that another helper, a man, shook back and forth. It looked like the archeologist was shaving the dirt with her shovel.

They found a few tiny items that looked like rocks. The lady said they could be important, and scooped them into a bag. They certainly weren't very exciting. Where were the arrow heads, the ancient pots? The dinosaur bones? They found nothing but dirt and small rocks. After a few hours Mary Beth's back hurt from bending over the screen, and there was dirt stuck under her fingernails. Her hands hurt from crumbling the cold dirt, and she couldn't see any difference between the pieces of rock and shell that they threw away and the ones they kept. She was very glad when Mom drove up and got out of the car with a basket for their lunch.

Mr. Niquette cupped his hands around his mouth and called out so that all the teams could hear. "Lunchtime! Back in an hour."

Some of the people left to go to restaurants but the archaeologist sat with Mary Beth and her friends. He ate the lunch he brought, while they ate the sandwiches and apples from their picnic basket.

He looked around at each of them as he chewed. "Well, what do you think of archaeology?"

They all looked at each other. Mary Beth didn't want to be rude, and she could tell by looking at her friend's face that Christy didn't either. David and Slicker concentrated very hard on their apples.

Mr. Niquette laughed. "Hard and boring work, huh?"

The kids all laughed too. Mary Beth relaxed as she took another bite of her sandwich. At least he knew how they felt.

He laid down his sandwich and jumped to his feet. "Let me show you something."

He got a book from a nearby pickup truck and brought it back to their picnic spot. Taking a seat beside Mary Beth, he opened the book. "Archaeology is a lot of hard work and much of the time it does seem boring. But by doing it, we find out things about the past. About the land and how it looked a long time ago, and especially about the people who lived then."

He pointed to a picture of a flat rock with one pointed end. "That unfinished spearhead was found on this very hill two years ago. That's why we are working here now. It was made, or partially made, about twelve thousand years ago. By sifting through the earth we can find out if it was dropped during travel or if someone camped here, or even if people camped here more than once." He grinned. "The job is more interesting if you play the 'What If' game."

"The 'What If' game?" Mary Beth asked.

"That's right." The archaeologist pointed to the picture again. "I look at this picture and I say to myself, 'What if this fell out of someone's pack and he was upset because he couldn't finish sharpening it and use it for hunting?'"

Slicker straightened, interest showing on his face. "And what if he starved because he couldn't kill anything to eat?"

Christy's eyes sparkled as she got caught up in the game. "And what if he had a daughter and she starved too?"

David was looking closely at the picture in the book. "What's this little hole in the spearhead?"

Mr. Niquette nodded, his lips forming a grin. "Very good observation. That little detail shows that my 'what if' is probably not true. What probably happened was that someone started forming that spearhead and got down to this section where acid or some other substance had damaged the rock, and realized it wouldn't be strong enough to use on his spear. So he threw it away." He looked around at the site. "But it shows that someone was here and tells us how long ago. And the work we are doing, with your help, will tell us a little more about them."

Mary Beth looked around the hillside. She could almost picture the girl Christy talked about. A lot of 'what if's' flew through her mind. One of them settled down and started to grow.

??? B.C.

The little girl could not remember a time when she was not cold, and tired. She knew she wanted fires and rest and food. There was something else she wanted, something she longed for, but she couldn't even form a picture in her mind of what it was. There was no word or sign in her language for the thing she wanted.

The little girl was called Ke, and she

lived with her mother and father and baby brother, her grandfather, her uncle and his wife, their son, and her aunt.

Ke's people never stayed anyplace for very long. All they knew, all their parents and grandparents had ever known, was to move southward ahead of the creeping mountains of ice, following the animals who provided the meat and skins they needed for food and clothes. Ke had spent all her life walking from one camp to another, helping set up cooking and sleeping places in a spot where they could choose stones to make weapons or cleaning tools, or a spot where they could hunt.

The hunting camps were always on a hill so the hunters could see the moose, caribou, or other game as they roamed the land. Ke wished they didn't have to camp on top of a hill because the wind was not so strong when they were below the hills. But no one ever asked Ke what she wished.

When they left their last camp, Ke had helped her father roll the tools and weapons into hides so they wouldn't be damaged on their journey. She liked to watch as her father carefully chose a stone and then began shaping it into a spearhead, or a tool to prepare meat or scrape hides. Her father was very good at making things.

Her grandfather was the best tracker. He knew just how to track a herd of bison or mammoth, and then where to corral them so they were easily caught. Ke worried sometimes about what would happen to them if her grandfather's spirit ever left them the way her grandmother's had done last year when they were crossing the frozen water. The ice gave way and though the family pulled Grandmother out of the water, she never opened her eyes again. Ke missed her, especially when she got a scrape or cut, or a burn from getting too close to the fire.

Grandmother had always known what leaves and roots to use to make everything feel better. Ke's aunt gathered those things for them now but Ke secretly thought that sometimes her aunt got them wrong because they didn't always work.

Ke's father and uncle hunted well, but they didn't always know where to find the herds like Grandfather did. Maybe her cousin would learn to be a

good tracker. He always watched closely to see what Grandfather was looking at before he made the decision where they would go next. It made Ke wish she'd paid more attention when Grandmother gathered her leaves and roots.

Ke's mother fixed most of their food, along with her uncle's wife. They gathered grain and pounded it to free it from the hard shells. When it was time to eat, they mixed it with water to make a paste. Sometimes the family ate it just like that, and sometimes they wrapped it around pieces of meat and held it over the fire pit until it formed a crust shell around the meat. Ke's favorite things to eat, when she wasn't too cold, were the juicy grapes they found hanging in clusters sometimes as they traveled.

Ke dressed in clothing her aunt made from caribou hide. Her mother's sister was the best among them at preparing the hides and them putting them together in a way that fit each person just right.

Ke's family all needed each other.

Today Ke was very tired and the longing for that thing she could not name was very strong. They had been several days traveling from the stone gathering site and she was ready for a camp where they would stay for a while and she could explore, and sleep in the same place for more than one night at a time. Her share of the load they carried from place to place was growing very heavy, and just as she thought she couldn't take one more step, Grandfather made a sound.

When Ke looked up, she saw a hillside ahead of them. A happy feeling spread through her. She'd seen Grandfather choose enough hunting sites to know that this was a place they would stay for a while.

When they reached the flat land at the top of the hill, Ke took a minute to look around before she started helping the family with the job of unpacking their supplies. It was a pretty land. Other hills, covered with the low sprawling bush-like trees she was so used to seeing, lay to the south. A stream surrounded by marshland lay to the west. Rolling meadows on the east would draw flocks and herds to the area. Yes, Grandfather had chosen well.

The hilltop was flat and sprawling, large enough for her family—and several other families—to camp there. The thought of many families camping together filled Ke with a great longing. They'd passed other families, each on their own journeys, and sometimes they even spent a night at the same site. But they never made camp together.

"What if...?" But Ke's longing could

think no further.

The next morning Ke helped her father unroll the pack of weapons. Some were finished and some not. He touched each of them tenderly, for every one represented many hours of work. He removed one spearhead that he'd begun work on a few days ago. He would finish it now, as they waited for the herds to come this way.

Ke watched as her father shaped the spearhead, flake by flake. Suddenly he made a gesture of disgust. A small hole appeared in the lower section. Something had damaged this piece and it would be no good to them. Even such a tiny hole would weaken the weapon. A shame, for already he had put a lot of work into it. He threw it aside and walked down the hill alone.

Everything the family carried had a purpose. But suddenly the rejected spearhead seemed to have a meaning to Ke, a purpose. Maybe if she kept it, she would remember this place and the moment when she sat with her father as he worked on it. And maybe that would help still the longing that she couldn't name. Ke picked up the damaged spearhead and slipped it into a fold of the hides she wore.

The family stayed many days on the

hill. The hunting was good, and Ke worked hard along with the others to prepare food and clothing and utensils. Every day when good things happened, Ke would secretly pat the spearhead hidden in the folds of her clothing and save that memory for the time when she would be in another place.

The day came when they were to leave. They must search for a site where they could gather rock and stone to replenish their store of weapons and tools. Ke hated to leave the hilltop where the family had so many good times, but with the spearhead to carry with her, she would never forget this place.

When everything was packed, the family started down the hill. Ke looked back and saw that nothing was left of their camp but ashes where the fire had been. The wind would blow the ashes away and there would be nothing left to show that she and the family had ever been there.

The spearhead felt heavy at her side and her heart started pounding. A new thought came to Ke. She could leave the spearhead here. And with it would be all the memories she had put in it. This place would be even more special when she thought back on it, because something of her would remain as she continued on her never-ending journey.

Moving quickly, she ran back up the hill and dug out a small hole in the loose dirt. She gently laid the spearhead in it and covered it over. When she raised her head, she saw that the family had stopped and were waiting for her. Giving the ground one final pat, she joined them.

Mr. Niquette lifted his head to scan the hilltop where Mary Beth and her friends sat finishing their lunch. "And what we are finding shows that this place was what we call a 'periodically revisited' camp. That means the people who first came here when the big glaciers stopped at the top of the state realized that they didn't have to move farther south.

"They never made a permanent home, but they did stay in the area, making temporary camps near places they could find rocks and hunt." The archaeologist closed the book. "The evidence shows that this spot was one where several tribes, or families, gathered on a regular basis to camp and hunt together."

"Oh, I'm so glad!" Mary Beth's excitement burst out even though she didn't mean it to.

The archaeologist looked at her with a twinkle in his eye as he stood to his feet. "Glad are you?"

Mary Beth's cheeks grew warm. It seemed like he knew how real her 'what if' had seemed to her. She nodded slowly.

"I'm glad too," he said. And winked

That afternoon the work was just as hard, but with the story of Ke fresh in her mind, Mary Beth enjoyed it. Maybe it wouldn't be so bad to be an archaeologist after all.

Adventure Two
Cumberland Gap

Slicker was fed up! He'd been looking forward to this trip for a long time and now it was spoiled.

He and David and their fathers had planned a camping trip to see some of the early places of Kentucky. They would start out near Winchester where the Shawnee once had a village, then go to Cumberland Falls and on to the place where Dr. Thomas Walker built the first cabin. They'd end up in Cumberland Gap where it all started, where Daniel Boone and the others came through the mountains to settle and run out the savage Indians. They were going to pitch tents and cook over an open fire and get the feel of pioneer days.

But no! Those stupid girls had to spoil everything. David's sister, Mary Beth, started begging to go. The next thing the boys knew, their mothers and Mary Beth and her friend, Christy, were included in the trip. And they weren't going to camp out. They had to stay in dumb old cabins and motels.

To top it all off, Mary Beth was showing off at Cumberland Falls State Park, climbed a tree and couldn't get down, and David sprained his ankle trying to help her. Their whole family left and went home. Slicker didn't care about Mary Beth and her Mom leaving but David and his Dad? Ugh.

The final blow came when they left Christy with his family. He had to bite back a groan when Mom said, "Oh, let Christy stay. I'm sure her parents won't mind. I'll watch out for her. And she will be company for Sidney."

Slicker hated the name Sidney, but his mother called him that anyway. His

Dad at least called him Sid. But he really wished they would call him Slicker.

He couldn't get the feel of being a pioneer with Christy following him around all the time, talking constantly.

"Look at this, Slicker."

"Why are you doing that, Slicker?"

"Where are you going, Slicker?"

"Wait for me, Slicker."

Here they were at the last place on their trip and he hadn't had a minute to himself. Yesterday at sunset, before they checked into the motel, they stood on Pinnacle Overlook and gazed out over the Cumberland River gleaming like a wide silver banner curling through the mountains.

Now Slicker looked out the motel window at dawn spreading over the tree-covered mountains. Oh, how he wanted to be in the middle of it. He glanced at his father sleeping—and snoring—on the double bed. His mom and Christy slept in the adjoining room.

One more day with that girl tagging behind him and he'd...he'd... well, he didn't know what he'd do, but he couldn't stand the thought.

He dressed quietly, folding his pajamas neatly and putting them on the dresser, so Mom would have one less thing to be angry about if she woke up before he got back. Then he slid the desk drawer open and took out the motel notepad.

> Dear Dad
>> Gone exploring
>> Back by 9
> Slicker

He put the note on top of the pajamas. Wait. Mom would blow a gasket when she read it. He tore up the note and started over. This time he signed it—Sidney. *She'll be upset with me, but at least that ought to make her happy.*

He closed the door without a sound and tiptoed down the hallway. And breathed a sigh of relief as he ducked around the back of the motel and into the woods.

He drew a deep breath. Had he ever smelled anything as fresh as the forest? The dew was thick on the undergrowth. Good thing he'd chosen to wear boots instead of Nikes. He'd brought his insulated bag and began picking up small bits of moss, fallen leaves, and wildflowers to take home, seal between waxed paper, and save to show his class at school.

A sound carried to him through the trees. Water running over rocks. Turning his head, he located the direction, followed the noise and came to a little creek. Where'd it come from? That would be a good goal for his morning exploration, to follow the creek upstream to find its source.

Slicker walked a long time, enjoying the quiet and fresh smells of the woods. Then he came to a stop. Nothing looked familiar. What part of the woods had he been in when he found the creek? The motel was south but how far east had he come? He looked at his watch and groaned. It was 8:30. He'd catch it for sure now.

All of a sudden the mountain forest didn't seem so exciting. He remembered all the tales he'd heard of savages and their attacks on the pioneers. Especially, he thought of Jamie Boone, the son of Daniel Boone. Jamie was a boy like himself who was tortured and killed not far from this very place.

Of course, Indians these days weren't angry with white settlers. Besides, they weren't in this area anymore. They moved west of the Mississippi River generations ago.

He backtracked a little way and

decided to start south through the woods. This time he notched the trees with his penknife as he went. Why didn't he do that when he left the motel? If he didn't see signs of the motel within ten minutes or so, he'd follow the notches back to the stream and go farther west before heading south again.

Suddenly his heart skipped a beat.

In front of him stood an Indian.

He was an old man, his skin heavy with wrinkles. He was dressed in jeans and a plain jacket, and wore boots, but he was an Indian, no doubt about that. He recognized the man's features from watching old cowboy movies with his Dad. With a mind full of raids and attacks, torture and scalping, Slicker could only stand frozen with fear.

He was shocked when the old man laughed. "Had any breakfast, son?"

Slicker swallowed hard and shook his head.

"Well, let's set a spell and remedy that." The old man took off his backpack and removed a large piece of plastic which he spread on the ground. He sat down and motioned for Slicker to sit beside him. Unable to move, Slicker watched while the Indian pulled out a small sack.

Goldfish crackers? Surely someone who ate Goldfish crackers couldn't be too awfully ferocious.

The Indian grinned. "I like 'em for breakfast."

Slicker nodded and sat down beside him on the tarp.

After they'd eaten two packages of Goldfish crackers each, Slicker felt relaxed. The old man explained that he was on vacation. He'd come from out west to see this land where his people once lived and hunted buffalo and other game. The beauty of the Cumberland and Kentucky was still spoken about among his people.

Before he knew he intended to, Slicker told him about how his own vacation had been spoiled by the girls.

The old man chuckled. "The oldest war." He nodded. "The war between male and female."

"Girls are dumb," said Slicker with disgust.

"Not so," said the Indian. "Only different." He grinned. "I bet you thought all Shawnee are bloodthirsty savages."

Slickers felt his eyes open wide. "Are you Shawnee?"

The old man nodded. His eyes took on a faraway look. "Seven fathers back, my ancestor Bear Paw lived north from here on the Little Miami River. In the year 1777, by white man's reckoning..."

Shawnee Village 1777

Bear Paw hoped The Grandmother was watching as he helped Little Running Deer out of the mud pit she fell in.

The Grandmother was not the mother of Bear Paw's mother, or the mother of his father. She was one of the two Guiding Spirits under The Great Spirit. The Grandmother was in charge of watching over the affairs of his people. Her grandson was the Spirit in charge of the lives of white men.

Bear Paw hated all white men and couldn't understand how The Grandmother could have a grandson who cared about them. But She did. And She let him take care of them.

Even now, Bear Paw's uncle and cousin were traveling to the Fort to warn the white men about discontent among the Shawnee. Bear Paw's uncle was Hokoleskwa, known as Cornstalk.

Cornstalk was the head chief over many villages of the Shawnee, and Bear

Paw's mother was one of the sub chiefs under him.

Bear Paw's mother didn't understand her brother's desire for peace with the whites. She'd taught Bear Paw since he was tiny how the whites were the cause of the Shawnee being driven out of their home in the Cumberland by the Iroquois, Cherokee, and the Chickasaw. She spat when she spoke the names of the other Indian people because they were 'lovers of the white man.' She said the Shawnee should have all the area south of where they lived now.

She also taught Bear Paw that the white man had killed his father before Bear Paw was even born.

Bear Paw was torn between love and respect for his uncle as a Chief and Warrior and hatred of Cornstalk's weakness where the white man was concerned.

If he were older, Bear Paw would not warn the hated white strangers. He would lead an attack on the fort. But Bear Paw was only twelve summers of age and had no power among his people. Yet.

His attention was brought back to the little girl now pulling on his arm. She was a pretty child, brown as a buckeye with a head properly flat in the back, showing that she'd been kept on a board during her first months to make sure she would grow straight and strong. She was now six summers and Bear Paw took special pride in her.

The family of Little Running Deer had their *wegiwa—or* wigwam—next to the wigwam of Bear Paw's family. He'd spent many hours sitting on the bench inside, watching the new baby as her eyes moved to learn and discover the world she had entered. He had only been six summers himself then.

The day she was allowed to be free from the board on which she spent her hours was a happy one for Bear Paw. And when she first crawled, it was straight to him. He hadn't been embarrassed at the laughter of his elders when he scooped her up in his arms and laughed with her in joy. He had determined then that she would be his squaw. For this reason, he was careful to please Red Eagle, her mother's brother, who would be the one to arrange her future marriage.

Bear Paw's only concern was that the family of Little Running Deer was too soft.

He sighed and looked where the girl was pointing, but he could see nothing.

"*Kewate*," insisted Little Running Deer, but Bear Paw saw no girl in the thicket across the stream. He turned back to the parched corn which he was pounding into flour for his mother.

Though this was women's work, Bear Paw often helped his mother. Their people were very proud of their corn crops, and his mother had the largest crop of them all. She was a busy woman. Besides growing and preparing food for herself and him, her only child, she had her duties as sub chief. She settled squabbles, set activities for the women, and was also the doctor of the village.

She was a strong willed woman and when Bear Paw was born, she overrode the family namegiver and named him herself.

He'd heard since he could remember how his people once lived in the far North but left there, separating themselves from the other tribes, when they were cheated out of some roasted bear paws at the end of a great hunt. They left and went south, becoming the Shawnee, the Southerners.

She named him Bear Paw, swearing eternal division between her people and the whites who killed her husband. Many were the verbal battles Bear Paw had heard between his mother and her brother.

Cornstalk said he hated the whites as much as she did, and he wanted the land of Kentucke more than she, for he could remember living there as a child at Blue Lick Place on the Great Warrior's Path to the south.

He recalled their father laboring to clear land for farming—land which had to be deserted. He also recalled their elders telling them that the Cumberland, even farther south, had rightfully been theirs and was now only a hunting paradise because of the white man's deception of other Indian tribes.

No, Cornstalk had no love for the whites. But he'd tried to explain to his sister that the whites were stronger both in number and in weapons. The Shawnee could not win. To fight would only mean that the Shawnee would all die.

Bear Paw's mother didn't believe it. And Bear Paw didn't believe it either. The Grandmother would watch over them. With every kind deed he did, Bear Paw asked The Grandmother to do something for the Shawnee.

His uncle, Cornstalk, had made peace with the whites three summers ago and promised that the Shawnee would stay north of the Ohio River. Bear Paw spat every time he thought of it. The other Shawnee thought as Bear

Paw did, and even now his uncle was warning the whites of the plans to break a treaty that they never agreed with.

Bear Paw looked upward and asked the Grandmother, "Please ruin that meeting. Don't let my uncle warn the enemy."

The corn was pounded to a fine powder now, which even his mother's keen eye would find no fault with. It would make a good bread, crusty on the outside, warm and moist inside, to go with the turkey and potatoes when she roasted them on the fire outside their wigwam.

Bear Paw suddenly looked around. He'd been so intent on his task and his thoughts that he'd not seen or heard Little Running Deer for some time. His heart lurched within him as his eyes swiftly searched the stream. Then he saw a flash of color through the thicket.

With his hand on the knife at his side, he leaped into the water and plunged through the trees. Little Running Deer stood in silence looking up at a woman. A white woman.

Bear Paw's fear for Little Running Deer and his hatred of all whites joined together in a fierce anger. In an instant, the knife was in his hand and raised into the air.

But Little Running Deer threw herself into the woman's arms. Through his rage, he could see that she was crying and holding out a small bunch of woodland flowers. Finally the roaring in his ears calmed enough for him to hear her words.

"No. Please. She is my friend. She gave me her flowers."

Bear Paw gritted his teeth as he clenched the knife with his fist. The woman's eyes pleaded with him as she clung to Little Running Deer. They would not have moved him. They were white eyes.

But Little Running Deer's eyes were pleading too. Finally Bear Paw lowered his arm. The child moved away from the woman and held his gaze with her own until the woman had retreated several yards.

The child whirled and ran after her while Bear Paw watched. She took the woman's hand and put it to her own chest. "Little Running Deer," she said.

She then put their clasped hands on the woman's chest and looked at her with widened eyes.

The woman gave a shaky little smile. "Bathsheba. Bathsheba Lincoln." And she leaned down and kissed the child on the forehead before disappearing into the brush.

Little Running Deer came back to where Bear Paw stood, and looked up at him with a determined look. "My friend," she said firmly.

She took his hand and they walked in silence back to the village.

"That was the last white person that Bear Paw ever showed mercy for." The old man shook his head sadly. "Word came back that Cornstalk and the others were murdered while on their peace mission. And even though the whites themselves called it an atrocity, the killers were never punished. Bear Paw led many raids against the whites and was finally killed during one of those attacks before he reached thirty summers."

The old man and the boy sat in silence under the trees on the mountain of the Cumberland.

Finally Slicker cleared his throat. "I can see why he hated us. What about Little Running Deer? Did he marry her?"

The Indian grinned. "My great-great-

great-great grandmother was both beautiful and wise. She taught their son that Cornstalk had been right. To fight the white man only ended in death. And she never forgot the white woman who gave her flowers and kissed her. She taught her son that some whites are kind. And grateful."

Slicker looked puzzled. "Bathsheba Lincoln. That's a strange name. Who was she?"

"The next year, 1778, Bathsheba Lincoln had a son, Thomas, who one day had a son named Abraham after his grandfather, Bathsheba's husband. She was the grandmother of the sixteenth president of the United States." The old man lifted his head proudly. "My family contributed to this nation."

Just then they heard the sound of rustling greenery from the direction Slicker had come. They sprang to their feet just as Slicker's dad and Christy came into the clearing.

His dad grinned and said. "We set out to find you and when we came to the creek, Christy said you'd try to follow it to its source. And then when we came to the first notch in the tree, she made me turn south and follow your trail."

"How'd you know?" Slicker looked at Christy with surprise.

Christy shrugged. "I've watched you a lot." Then she smiled like she knew what he'd been thinking about her following him around. "I'm starting to know how you think."

Slicker remembered his manners and introduced his Dad and Christy to his Indian friend. After he and his Dad thanked the man for sharing his breakfast and visiting with Slicker, the three headed back to the motel and Mom, following the notches Slicker's Dad had made.

Mom wasn't as ready to brush off his adventure as Dad had been but since they were on vacation, her frowns and lecture was the only punishment.

Slicker had to admit that Christy's excitement when she told his Mom about the adventure and his Indian friend might have helped him escape worse consequences. Maybe a girl could be a friend after all.

Adventure Three
Fort Harrod

"**W**hat is wrong with you, Christy?" Mary Beth was worried. It wasn't like her best friend and lifelong next door neighbor to be so quiet. Especially when they were in the middle of one of their adventures.

The girls had been looking forward to this trip to Harrodsburg for weeks. Mary Beth's brother David and his best friend, Slicker, were staying in a motel room with her father, and Mary Beth and Christy had a motel room with Mom. They would take a tour of Fort Harrod this afternoon and go to eat at nearby Shakertown for supper. They were going to learn a lot more things about their state on this trip. But now they were here and Christy was quiet and didn't seem at all glad.

"I really don't want to talk about it," said Christy, laying the hairbrush down on the motel dresser.

Mary Beth was speechless. Christy not wanting to talk about something! To her best friend? The girls had told each other everything all their lives. There must really be a serious problem. Before Mary Beth could think of anything to say, her mother came back into the room.

"Are you girls ready to go? The men are chomping at the bit."

"David and Slicker aren't men." Christy spoke in a low voice.

Mary Beth glanced at her Mom, who looked as shocked as she was. It was not like Christy to correct an adult. She was always very polite. Mary Beth's mother walked over to Christy.

"Do you feel all right?" She put her hand on Christy's forehead, like she always did to Mary Beth when she thought she might be running a fever. "You don't seem hot."

Immediately Christy sat down on the bed and started crying. Mary Beth's mother sat down beside her and put her arms around the sobbing girl.

"What's wrong, Christy? If you tell me, maybe I can help."

Christy just shook her head and kept on crying.

Mary Beth's mother looked up and caught her eye. "Would you run next door and tell your Dad that Christy and I will be a few minutes longer? You can stay there until we join you." And the look added, "Don't say anything is wrong and embarrass Christy."

As if she would! Mary Beth didn't slam the door very hard when she left.

⁕ ⁕ ⁕ ⁕ ⁕

When they were alone, Christy cried for a few more minutes. She didn't want to betray her own parents, but Mary Beth's Mom was so comforting. And she really needed to talk to somebody. "I think my Mom and Dad are getting a divorce," she blurted out between sobs.

"Oh, no. You must be mistaken.

Your parents love each other very much. I'm sure of it."

"B...but last night I heard them talking. They thought I was asleep but I got up to get a drink of water. Mom was crying and they said something about selling the house." Christy sobbed. "And that's what happens with kids at school when their parents get a divorce. Their mothers cry and they sell the house."

Mrs. Thompson looked like she might be holding back a smile, but Christy hoped she wasn't going to laugh at her.

"Christy, there can be many reasons for selling a house—money problems, to get a bigger house, lots of reasons. And believe me," she tilted Christy's face up to look at her, "most mothers cry sometimes and it almost never means a divorce."

Christy wanted to believe her. Maybe she was right. Mom did cry sometimes, for lots of different reasons. But Christy still wanted to be at home, to make sure that everything was all right. And she didn't want a bigger house. They couldn't make a decision like that without her. They just couldn't!

Mrs. Thompson gave her shoulders

a final hug. "Come on now, let's get your face washed and go meet the others. You'll feel better when we get to the fort."

Christy didn't think so, but she did as she was told.

Mary Beth was really quiet as they drove, and also after they got to Fort Harrod. Christy knew she had hurt her friend's feelings and she was sorry. But she didn't know what to say to make things better. Things weren't better.

She barely heard what Mr. Thompson said about the fort while they were going through it. Her mind was full of 'what if's', not about the fort but about her family. It couldn't be a bigger house. They would ask her about that. Her parents must be having money problems. Mrs. Thompson was right. Mom and Dad did love each other. And she'd heard something mentioned about her Dad's job. What was it? She hadn't heard what was said, just the words 'my job.'

Oh no! Dad lost his job. She'd heard grownups talk about jobs and how so many people didn't have them these days. If you didn't have a job, you didn't have any money.

They were going to be poor.

They would have to sell the house.

They wouldn't have enough to eat.

She would have to wear rags.

She'd read stories about people who had no money. Her parents would die of starvation and she would have to sell matches on the street and then she would die of starvation too.

She followed the others from one log building into another, this one an old schoolhouse. While Mary Beth's father told them about the building, she sank onto a log bench. Mr. Thompson explained about the fireplace and how it had a big hole at the side so they could put a long log in it from the outside. When part of it was burned, they could push it in farther and burn another part of it. That way they didn't have to keep carrying more logs in. It seemed like a good idea, but Christy was too worried to concentrate.

"Are you coming, Christy?" Mary Beth's mother smiled gently as they all started out the doorway.

"In a minute," she said.

When they had gone, she stared at the dirt floor and wondered about the children who sat here two centuries ago learning to read and write and do arithmetic. With her heel, she drew a C for her name in the dirt.

Maybe she and her parents would

move to a place with a dirt floor and only a fireplace for heat. She'd have to tell them about that hole for a big log. Life was going to be awful. If only she were home to find out what was really going on.

"I don't want to be here. I don't want to be here." She wasn't sure if she just thought it or said it out loud.

Fort Harrod 1784

"I don't want to be here. I don't want to be here." The words flew round and round in Rebecca's head as she stared at the backs of the children's heads on benches in the schoolhouse.

How she hated them. They were stupid and dirty and ... she couldn't even think of words bad enough. How could they giggle and act silly when they were all in danger, when their fathers—and hers—were missing, maybe badly hurt? Or even dead.

At the thought of her father, tears sprang to Rebecca's eyes, but she quickly wiped them away with the back of her hand. She would never let those others see her cry.

She and her mother had been here

at James Harrod's fort for four weeks now. They were staying at Mrs. Lindsay's. It had been bad enough when they were in their own cabin, at their own station. Her mother often cried and talked about her parents' home in Pennsylvania.

Grandmother's house had glass windows and gleaming wood floors with thick carpets, carved mantles and banisters, and teacups you could hold up to the light and see the outline of your hand through. Mother's voice filled with longing as she talked about soft beds and buildings just to do the wash in—and servants to do it for you. But most of all she talked about people who said *only* instead of *onliest,* and *youngest child* instead of *least un,* people who read good books and played beautiful music.

Oh, they'd left behind so many things when Rebecca's father decided to move west to Kentucke. Or Kaintuck. Or Kentucky. These people didn't even know what to call the place where they lived. The town near the fort was called Harrodstown by some and Harrodsburg by others. Stupid, stupid, stupid! And even too stupid to know they were stupid.

At least when Rebecca and her

family were in their own station, awful though it was with dirt floors and skins stretched over the windows, and only one room and a loft, at least it was quiet. She could play with her doll and her mother could read when the work was done. But here the work was never done.

Her father came to Kentucky before they did. And they were surprised, not a happy surprise, when he came back and told them he'd bought land, and had a home almost finished for them to live in. Rebecca's grandparents begged him to change his mind but he wouldn't. Then they begged their daughter to stay there with them.

Rebecca still remembered the look on her father's face as he waited for her mother's decision. And she remembered the joy that made him look no older than she was, when her mother said that she and Rebecca belonged with him.

So here they were. When they arrived at the fort last year, Rebecca was horrified. She and her mother stayed a week while her father and some other men finished their cabin and put up the wooden fence that

made a barricade around it. It was all so different and crude and loud in the fort. How glad they all were to leave, even to live in the cabin. But now they were back.

Last month a rider came and told them of trouble with the Indians. Rebecca and her mother wanted to stay in the cabin and take their chances, but Rebecca's father said he had to go help put a stop to the threat for all of them. He couldn't let the others do all the fighting and protecting while he stayed at home. And he couldn't go away and leave his wife and child alone. So back to the fort they came, into the noise and the dirt and the...the...the awfulness!

The other children in the school room stood. It must be lunch time. Mrs. Coomes walked back to where Rebecca sat waiting for the others to leave. The teacher smiled down at her.

"Rebecca, I am coming with you for the mid-day meal this noon. Your mother and Ann Lindsey have invited me."

Rebecca nodded. Mrs. Coomes was really not a bad person. She started the first school in this awful place. She was trying to make things better. And she did know about books and things, even if they had to learn from boards that looked like a paddle. The teacher made them herself. She wrote the alphabet and the Lord's prayer on them with berry juices, one for each child. You had to admire her for that. And she didn't say *onliest*.

They walked in silence across the center of the fort to Ann Lindsay's blockhouse in the corner. Most of the people here lived in stations like Rebecca's family. Only those who were leaders of the fort lived here full time. Mrs. Lindsay was in charge of all the women's activities. Rebecca had never seen so much energy in a woman—or a man either for that matter.

Mrs. Lindsay invented a new kind of cloth when the fort was first settled nine years ago and there wasn't enough wool to make clothes for everybody. Her husband built the first loom in Kentucke. She had been Mrs. Poague then, and Rebecca heard that William Poague had been her second husband! Back in Pennsylvania, no woman ever had three husbands. She didn't think her grandmother would approve of Mrs. Lindsay.

When they entered the blockhouse, Mrs. Lindsay was just taking the spider off the fire. The spider was an iron skillet on legs that got its name because it looked kind of like a spider. This time it was full of cornbread. Though Rebecca still missed the light fluffy biscuits back in Pennsylvania, she was getting used to the crusty bread.

Mother was ladling stew from the kettle into bowls. Rebecca snuck up behind and put her hands over her mother's eyes.

"Guess who?" It had been their game ever since Rebecca could remember.

"Rebecca! Be careful. You'll make

me spill the stew."

Her sharp tone stung Rebecca's feelings. Even Mother wasn't the same when they were at the fort. She sat in silence while everybody talked through the meal.

"We get this Indian business settled," Mrs. Lindsay said, "I'm gonna start me a Ordinary." Her eyes sparkled. "I kin just see it. This country's gonna grow, and I aims to do well. Folks'll be comin' from all over and they're gonna need somewhere to board while they're choosin' a place and settlin' in."

Mrs. Coomes nodded and Rebecca turned to exchange that secret look that she and her mother had when the others did or said strange things. But her mother was watching Mrs. Lindsay. Was that a spark of interest in her eyes?

"What do you think, Jane?" Mrs. Lindsay asked Rebecca's teacher.

Jane Coomes smiled her slow, sweet smile that had a touch of mischief in it. "I think that if anyone could make a success of an Ordinary, it would be you."

Everyone knew she didn't just mean Mrs. Lindsay was a good cook. If Mrs. Lindsay wanted something, she worked hard, and bullied other people, until she got it.

Rebecca sank low in her chair. Mrs. Lindsay bossed her mother all the time. She'd insisted on teaching her how to make lye soap. What would Grandmother say if she saw her daughter's hands now? And she made her learn to make candles and even carve things out of wood. How could her mother be sitting there looking kindly at that woman?

Father and the others better get back soon so her family could go back to—she couldn't make herself call it home—their cabin.

Home. That was Pennsylvania with real streets and pretty clothes and all the things that made life good. Maybe after being away from them for so long, her father would see that they should go home, away from all this fear and dirt and discomfort.

Suddenly someone appeared in the doorway. One of the older boys. He shouted, "They're back!"

Mother grabbed her hand and they followed the others outside. The big gate was open and men were pouring into the fort. Dirty men. Wounded men. Loud men.

Rebecca was proud that her mother

walked slowly. Some of the women were running, the men picking them up and swinging them around. She was glad her father was not like that. When he came through the gate, he would walk over to them and smile his gentle smile at her mother, and then at her. And they would all be glad but they would act dignified.

But Father did not come through the gate.

Their second month in the fort was worse than the first. The men told Mother that they had all been separated. Some had been killed but no one knew what happened to Father. He might have been captured by the Indians, or he might have been killed and they just hadn't found his body.

Mother didn't cry as much as Rebecca thought she would. Or should. And she didn't pack their things and insist on a guide back to Pennsylvania. She just got quieter, except at night when Rebecca could hear her talking with Mrs. Lindsay. Their voices were too low to understand.

Only one time did Rebecca know what they were talking about and that was because her mother raised her voice.

"No! A few years ago maybe that custom was necessary. But not now. Rebecca and I can make it." Her mother's voice came up through the boards of the loft floor. Rebecca sat straight up on the straw mattress. Make it? What could she mean? If Father didn't come, they would go back home. They wouldn't need to 'make it.' Surely her mother couldn't be thinking about staying here without Father.

"Well, maybe you're right. When I get my Ordinary goin'..." Then the voices got quiet again and Rebecca couldn't hear any more.

She was shaking, even though the night was very hot. Stay here in the fort? Forever? It was too awful to even think about. That woman was ruining Mother. Rebecca forced herself to breathe. At least Mother said "Rebecca and I can make it." and that meant she wasn't going to marry one of those men who started hanging around as soon as they got back.

That was one reason Rebecca had been so sure they would leave for Pennsylvania immediately. The other children told her that no woman could stay there without being married. And they had to choose a husband after one month from when their husband was killed or disappeared.

"What if their real husband comes back?" Rebecca had asked the question because her mother kept telling her that Father would be back any day now.

The children told her. "Then they gets to pick which they wants. The first 'un or the new 'un."

At first she thought they were teasing her. But when she questioned Mrs. Coomes, the lady looked troubled as she admitted that was the custom.

"When an area is being settled for the first time, dear, there are often things that must be done which wouldn't be done in normal times or places."

No, the children weren't teasing her. And as the weeks went by, Rebecca began to see that they really cared about her and her mother. One boy made a noggin—a cup hollowed out from the knot of a tree—for her so she could dip water from the spring. That sweet gesture left Rebecca's heart in turmoil. Yes, the people here seemed friendlier. Or was she just getting used to them?

Still, everything was worse because Father wasn't there. Was he ever coming back? Every day Mother's interest in their surroundings brought home a terrible truth—they were never going back to Grandmother's. This was their new life. Rebecca was just going to have to learn to accept it.

One afternoon Rebecca raised her hand in class and Mrs. Coomes nodded that she could be excused. The spring wasn't far from the schoolhouse. She wasn't really thirsty, but wanted to be alone for a while. The sun sparkled overhead as she made her way to the stream. She pulled the noggin out of her pocket and dipped it into the cool water. When she first arrived in Harrodstown, the other children had warned her against 'Old Barney' whose headless ghost was said to haunt the spring. Mrs. Coomes told her that Old Barney's ghost was just something the children made up to help make things more exciting during the long, boring stay in the fort.

It was a quiet afternoon and the wildflowers in the grass made Rebecca wonder how the seeds her mother gave her to plant outside their cabin were growing. It seemed like a lifetime ago, but it had only been eight weeks. She sat down on the ground, not caring for once if she got stains on her dress. Grandmother would never see it anyway.

She was deep in thought a noise reached her. When she looked up, she couldn't believe her eyes. Her very quiet mother was running and screaming. The fort's gate was open and a tall man dashed inside, yelling. He grabbed Mother in his arms and swung her around, both of them laughing and crying. Everybody in the fort seemed to be outside cheering. It was not dignified at all.

Then the man put her mother down and looked around. Rebecca's heart felt like it stopped.

Father!

She didn't care about anything else in the world except running to him, laughing and crying just like Mother. And then she was scooped up in his arms and her heart felt like it might burst right inside her chest.

She and Father and Mother all hugged each other while the other children formed a circle around them, skipping and singing. The grownups were all talking at the same time. Rebecca heard Mrs. Lindsay's voice through all the noise.

"Yer takin' away my first real full-time help, but I shore am glad."

Mrs. Coomes brushed away tears

and nodded at them all.

"We'll go home tomorrow." Father smiled down at Rebecca and Mother.

All of a sudden, Rebecca knew where home was. It was wherever her family could be together. If that home was in Kentucky, fine with her. A new home in a new land. She looked around at all the faces surrounding them. At least in Kentucky they had neighbors who cared and who were always there when you needed them.

And most of all, they had each other.

***

"Christy! Christy, wake up!"

Christy's face felt funny from laying on the rippled surface of the log bench. Someone was shaking her arm. Mary Beth's mother. She turned to speak to someone standing in the doorway to the schoolhouse.

"I'm a little worried about her. She hasn't been feeling well today. That's why I called you."

Christy sat up. Two people entered the log building. It was Mom and Dad! She jumped to her feet and ran to them, hugging them both at the same time.

Before she could stop herself, her worry tumbled out. "You're not going to get a divorce, are you?"

Both of her parents looked surprised, and then they laughed.

"Of course not." Dad rumpled her hair the way she loved. "What's this all about?"

Christy's friends filed in, expressions curious, and stood near the back of the schoolhouse. Christy looked down at the dirt floor. "I was awake last night and heard you talking about selling the house. And Mom was crying." She looked up, smiling through a sudden flood of tears. "But it's okay. I don't care about being poor as long as we stay together."

Dad sat down on one of the log benches and pulled her down on his knees. "Christy Bear." Christy was so glad to be on his lap that she didn't mind the pet name in front of the others. "I was offered a job with more money in another state. We were talking about that. But your mother and I decided we don't want to leave our home and our friends." He smiled and looked around at Mary Beth and her parents and David and Slicker, who were standing silently near the back of the schoolhouse.

"I'm glad." Christy nodded solemnly. "Neighbors are important, you know."

"I know." Dad's expression became serious. "Something else is important too. If there's something you want to know from Mom and me, you should always come and ask. Good or bad, we'll tell you the truth. Promise from now on you will ask?"

"Promise," said Christy, and hugged his neck.

The rest of the day was wonderful. When she realized what had been bothering Christy, Mary Beth's feelings weren't hurt anymore. And Mom and Dad finished going through the fort with them, and joined them at Shakertown for dinner.

At the hotel that night Mom joined the 'ladies room' as Dad called it, which made the girls giggle. Dad spent the night in the 'gentlemen's room.' The day couldn't have ended better.

Christy slid beneath the covers and snuggled up to Mom. As sleep crept over her, she gave a happy sigh. She knew exactly how her 'what if' dream girl, Rebecca, felt. Even in this hotel room, she felt at home because she was with the people she loved.

Adventure Four
Constitution Square

"**B**oring, boring, boring." Mary Beth kicked the tree root by her feet. "I'd rather go to the neighborhood cookout."

"Me too," agreed Christy, her shoulders slumped.

"Me too." Slicker sounded like a man on a chain gang being led off to prison.

David reached up and grabbed a handful of leaves from a low-hanging branch. The others sure were acting grumpy. With a grin he tossed the leaves in Slicker's direction and watched them rain down on his head. "We'll make it fun."

They all looked at him like he was crazy. The four friends were in Mary Beth and David's back yard talking about the plans for the Fourth of July holiday. Their parents told them that morning they would all be going to an Independence Day celebration at Constitution Square in Danville tomorrow. They had been looking forward to the annual neighborhood cookout with sack races and softball and lots of other games with their neighbors.

"Really," insisted David. "It could be fun. Remember how we've made adventures out of all the other places we've visited?"

"But they were fun places anyway." Mary Beth glared at him.

Slicker raised his eyebrows at her. "Like the archeological dig?"

Mary Beth blushed and David couldn't stop a grin. She'd hated that archeological dig at first. But by the end of the day she loved it.

"What could possibly be fun about making a state constitution?" Christy folded her arms and joined Mary Beth in glaring.

David thought a few seconds. "I admit it doesn't sound very exciting but let's make the trip an experiment."

A flicker of interest showed on their faces.

"What kind of experiment?" asked Slicker.

"We'll play the 'what if' game."

Christy scowled. "David, we studied those conventions in school, all ten that they held before Kentucky finally became a state. Don't you remember? Not even a 'what if' could make them interesting."

Slicker spoke up. "She's right, David. I could hardly stay awake in class when we studied that part of Kentucky history."

"We have to go anyway." David shrugged. "It can't hurt. Here's what we'll do..."

The next morning was a bright sunshiney day. When they arrived at the Square, people were setting up booths with souvenirs and other things to sell. Two men were putting up microphones and speakers on a stage set up on one side of the open area near some old-looking log buildings. The three families ate lunch on picnic tables and then wandered through the buildings.

Dad liked history a lot and David could tell he enjoyed being their guide and explaining about all the buildings. They looked into the first post office in the west, which had been moved from a few blocks away to stand here in the park. And the 'meeting house' that had been a Presbyterian Church under the leadership of a man named Reverend David Rice. There was the jail which had one side for debtors and one side for real criminals.

They saw the Courthouse where the ten conventions had been held, and Grayson's Tavern where all the men from miles around stayed and ate and talked. Dad explained that the first constitutional convention was in 1784 and finally the tenth one led to Kentucky becoming a state in 1799. The kids already knew this but they listened politely.

Finally the tour was over and the adults sat down at a table to wait for the entertainment to start. David nodded to the others to follow him.

When they were crowded in the meeting house away from everybody, Christy said, "See? Boring, boring, boring, just like we thought."

David planted his hands on his hips. "Come on, Christy, you agreed to try."

"Oh, all right." But she narrowed her eyes at David as they split up, each heading toward different buildings.

After a while, the children met back in the picnic area. They chose a table on the opposite end of the square from their parents so they could talk without being overheard. Their expressions were very different from when they parted and David was relieved. Maybe his plan had worked.

Excitement sparkled in Christy's eyes. "Can I be first?" David nodded.

"I went to Grayson's Tavern. And in the kitchen right behind the tavern..."

⁂

Danville, Kentucky 1788

"Dem white gemplemums shore do yell a lot. I didn't get no sleep last night and Mista James didn't either. "

Rachel grinned at the little boy. "If

you aren't a slave, you better stop talking like one. Gemplemums!"

"I told you, I ain't no slave." Mose's dark eyes flashed. "And Mista James gonna teach me. I'm gonna learn to read and write and ... well, and everthing."

Rachel giggled. She was eleven and helped her mother in the kitchen of Ben Grayson's tavern. It was hot and boring work, especially in July. The Negro boy made life a little more interesting since his arrival two days ago with Mr. Birney, who planned to settle in Danville and open a business in the fall. Mose came to the kitchen and talked to her while she peeled vegetables and washed plates.

The tavern was full from the visitors here for the convention but Mr. Grayson found room for the man and boy in a storage place behind the big sleeping room upstairs.

"What's them gemplemums...what you s'posed to call 'em?"

"Gentlemen." Rachel dried her hands on her apron and picked up a basket of potatoes. "Those gentlemen."

"Gentlemen." He repeated the word carefully. "What's them, I mean those, gentlemen so fired up about?"

"Ma says it's about freedom." Rachel

set the potatoes on the table and picked up a knife.

"I knows about freedom." Mose nodded. "Two years ago I was a slave, me 'n my daddy. And we couldn't do nuffin or go nowhere. And then 'ol Massa, he died and Daddy said he did have no hair so Daddy reckoned we was free and we just lit out. Tho I don't see what 'Ol Massa being bald had to do with it."

Rachel whooped with laughter.

"What you laughin' at?" The little boy squinted at her and Rachel could see that she'd hurt his feelings, so she made herself quit laughing and go on peeling potatoes.

"Not hair. *Heir*. It means the person who gets all the things you own when you die. Your master didn't have an heir so your daddy figured you and he would be sold at an auction. Maybe he decided to take you and leave. Where were you going, Canada?"

Mose's face brightened. "Yeah. Mista James asked me where we was headin' and I couldn't remember. But that's it. That's what mah daddy said. Canada."

Rachel softened her voice. "What happened to your daddy?"

Tears sprang to Mose's eyes. "He done got kilt. Some mean men saw us 'n started yellin' and chasin' us and they got my daddy but I hid out in the woods. That's where Mista James foun' me. He did some checkin' and found out them men done kilt Daddy. So he said I could come with him and help him in his store." The boy straightened his shoulders proudly. "I'm gonna be a storekeeper."

Rachel smiled at the boy. "I guess you do know about freedom. Well what's going on here, what all the gentlemen are upset about, that's about freedom too."

Mose's eyes widened. "Them white gemp—gentlemen, they're not slaves, is they? I never heard of no white slave."

"No, they're not slaves." She placed a peeled potato in the bowl. "But Ma says that most of those men helped fight so this country could be free from the king back in England telling us what to do. Now the government in Virginia tells us what to do and they're so far away they don't know what we need." All the potatoes were peeled. She set the knife on the table. "So, the gentlemen have been meeting to talk about making Kentucky a state, not just a district of Virginia. Then they'll be able to decide things on their own, like how to fight the Indians and where is best to trade and stuff like that."

"But what are they yellin' about?"

Rachel poured water over the potatoes and threw the peelings in a basin with the other things to feed to the hogs. "I guess they're frustrated. They've been meeting for over three years. This is the sixth time they've been here. Ma said they thought it was all fixed and now they found out they were too late. The deadline had passed, so we're still not a state." She sighed. "I wish they'd get it over with, so I wouldn't have so much work to do."

Mose jumped down off the stool. "I better get back to Mista James. He might need me." He started out the door and then turned back. "I hope you gets to be a state so you can be free."

Rachel smiled at him. "I thought you were going to stay here and be a shopkeeper. You better hope *we* get to be a state."

❀ ❀ ❀ ❀

"Wow," Slicker nodded. "That makes the convention stuff more interesting."

David said, "You know I went to the Courthouse. It was April of 1792 when the final constitution was being written.

Danville, Kentucky 1792

Pride swelled big in Mose's chest. This was the first time the baby would be going out and Miz Martha asked him to walk with them to get some tonic from Dr. Rankin. The baby sure hadn't been pretty the first time Mose saw it, but now he was two months old and starting to look like a real human being.

"You sure you don't need me, Mista James?" he asked the Irishman behind the counter.

"I always need you, Mose. You're the best help any storekeeper could have." Mista James grinned at him. "But you go on with Miss Martha and little James. I'll feel better about them taking their first walk since he was born if I know you are there to take care of them."

Mose nodded. Mista James was always telling him how much they all needed him. He would laugh and put his arm around Mose while he told customers how he'd never have made the store a success if it weren't for Mose.

Back in the days when they started the store, it had been just the two of them. When Mista James started calling on Miz Martha, Mose hadn't been sure he liked the idea. But it all worked out and now he couldn't decide which one he loved most. And then came this new little one to love. Mose couldn't remember his own mother and he'd never been around any little babies. He decided he liked this new world of ladies and babies.

After they got the tonic, Miz Martha suggested they walk up to the square and see what was going on. Mose was glad. When he first came to Kentucky, it looked like they would never get their freedom and become a state. His daddy'd told him that freedom was the most important thing in the world. And now it had all worked out and Virginia was going to let Kentucky go. President George Washington himself had said Congress should let Kentucky be a state. Now all they had to do was write up a con... con...

"What's that thing they're makin', Miz Martha?" Mose asked as they reached the square.

"Constitution, Mose. It's where they agree on the laws this new state will have, and what rights the people in it will have."

"What's that mean?"

"Well," Miz Martha paused to peek inside the blanket at her sleeping baby. "I know they decided something that none of the other states have decided. In Kentucky you won't have to have a certain religion or own property to be able to vote. All white men twenty-one years old can vote."

Mose wrinkled his brow. "Me and you can't vote, Miz Martha?" What kind of freedom was that?

"No. Not women and not Negroes." Miz Martha was quiet for a long time. There were a few people walking around the square. She nodded a greeting as they passed a pair of older ladies.

Finally she asked, "Mose, do you say your prayers like I taught you to?"

"Yes'm, ever night when I go to bed."

"Mose, I want you to pray for Father Rice and the other ministers here at the convention. They are trying to have it made a part of Kentucky's law that no one is a slave here."

Mose was so surprised he almost stopped walking to stare at her. "No slaves? None at all?" Back when he was little living on the plantation he saw a slave on a nearby farm tied to a post and beaten 'til he died. Then there were those men who chased him and his daddy, calling them runaway slaves. No slaves would mean no killings.

"No slaves," he repeated in awe.

"Not in Kentucky," said Miz Martha. "Not if they put it in the constitution. So you pray for them, you hear?"

Mose nodded. "Miz Martha, we really would be free then, wouldn't we? Free all the way through?" The thought made him feel glad way down deep inside. He repeated it. "Free all the way through."

* * *

"Oh, I hope they did!" cried Christy. "A brand new state with freedom all the way through. Did they do it, David?"

David shook his head. The truth made him sad. "No. In fact they got so mad at the ministers they made it a law that ministers couldn't be in public office."

Slicker had been wiggling around the whole time David was telling his 'what if.'

"Did you want to go next, Slicker?" David asked, even though he knew the answer.

"Yes. I went to the jail like you told

me...."

Danville, Kentucky 1799

Benji was scared. James and Mose talked him into coming with them but if they got caught he'd get a whipping as sure as they would.

It was dark. His parents and Mr. and Mrs. Birney thought they were all safely in bed. It was cold too. March nights could be almost like January when it came to cold.

Mose and James were arguing, in whispers of course.

"It's all right, Mose," James said. "If we get caught, I'll tell them I made you come with me. To protect me. I'll tell them I was coming with or without you."

Mose shook his head. "I don't think Miz Martha 'n Mista James will believe that. They'll say 'Mose you are seventeen years old and Mista James G, he's only seven. You should've waked us up.' That's what they'll say. And they'll be right."

James ignored Mose and kept right on walking like he hadn't said a word. Benji stayed hard on James' heels.

Following behind him, Mose's resigned sigh sounded loud in the quiet night.

In a few minutes, their destination appeared in front of them.

"There it is. There's the jail." Benji's whisper was a little louder than he meant for it to be. His heart was pounding. Why had he let his neighbor talk him into sneaking out with them? Even though James was the youngest, he always seemed to get his way.

"What's wrong with you two?" James sounded disgusted, even in a whisper. "This may be our only chance to see a real live murderer."

"I saw murderers aplenty when I was little," muttered Mose.

"Hush!" Benji was really scared now. "We don't want them to hear us."

The boys walked as quietly as they could, one foot in front of the other, the way they'd heard that Indians walked. They rounded the corner of the jail and very slowly slipped up to the window.

When it was his turn to look in, Benji eased up from a crouch, just high

enough to peek inside. There was a fire
in the fireplace, though the light it cast
was too dim to see much. A woman
stood near it rubbing her hands, and
another woman sat on a cot making
soft noises to two babies lying there. A
third woman paced back and forth with

another baby, who was fussing.

Two men sat at a table. Both had a foot chained to the ground.

Disappointment flooded through him. *This* is what they risked their necks to see?

James motioned for him and Mose to follow him a short distance away.

"Big Harpe's the one with two wives and two babies. Little Harpe just has one of each. Wonder which is which?"

"You ready to go now, Mista James?" Mose whispered. "There ain't nothing more to see."

"He's right." Benji nodded. "Let's go."

"Not yet," James insisted.

The whole town had talked about nothing else since January when Big and Little Harpe and their three wives were brought to the jail to wait for their trial in April. And all three women had their babies right there in the jail. The men were there because they had murdered a man right outside of Crab Orchard. That little town didn't have a jail so they brought the bunch to Danville by horses and buggies. Everybody said the Harpes were mean as snakes and liked to kill people just for the fun of it.

A baby started to cry. The boys crept back to the window.

The bigger man said to the smaller one, "You better make yore woman keep that kid quiet or I'm gonna kill it." The woman who had been walking the fussy baby walked faster and talked louder to try to hush the crying infant.

"Poor baby." James' whisper was quiet as a mouse nibbling cheese.

But not quiet enough.

The chair fell over as Big Harpe jumped to his feet. "Who's out there?" His roar made Benji jump nearly out of his shoes. "I'll skin you alive when I get outta here. Won't have people spyin' on me!"

Benji didn't wait to see if James was going to answer. He ran across the square as fast as he could, toward his home and his warm bed.

But he guessed James didn't tell because he heard two sets of feet running right behind him.

"I wonder what happened to them all." Christy looked thoughtful.

David glanced at his sister, who had been quiet for a long time. She wore a sour expression, and didn't meet anyone's eye. "You haven't shared your 'what if,' Mary Beth."

"I don't want to." Mary Beth sounded angry. "I like happy endings. I don't like this 'what if' at all!"

The others all protested at the same time. They'd told their stories. It wasn't fair for her not to tell hers. David cocked his head and studied her. Was her 'what if' going to have the same people in it as theirs? And how did that happen anyway? Since they'd all studied Kentucky history, maybe they'd come across the names of Mose and James somewhere, so they all conjured them up in their imaginations. But it was kind of creepy how they all pictured the same people in their 'what if' stories.

"Oh, all right." She planted her elbows on the table in front of her. "You know I went to the post office and no wonder I couldn't get into the right time. I mean the times of the conventions. The post office didn't even start until the fall after Kentucky became a state. And it wasn't on the square. It's all so confusing. It was way later..."

Danville, Kentucky 1835

Kitty's hand tightened around Gramps' fingers. He was right to be angry with her. She shouldn't have followed him here. But Gramps was her favorite person in the whole world.

Most times he didn't care if she tagged along. They made a game out of it. He'd pretend he didn't know she was there and say out loud, like he was talking to himself, "I believe I smell the footprints of a woozle on my trail." Then Kitty would giggle because there wasn't any such thing as a woozle and you didn't smell footprints, you saw them.

Then Gramps would turn around and swing her up on his shoulders and she would ride high above everybody, like a queen, and go with him everywhere he went.

But today he'd been different. He hadn't played the game at all. He'd scowled at her, and scolded. "Kitty! I told you to stay home with your grandmother."

She was so shocked at his harsh tone that she didn't know what to say. Then Gramps took her hand. "Well, I'm just going to be a minute. Want to hear what's going on. But you be still, you mind?"

Kitty nodded. They were about a

block from the post office when they heard angry voices. She began to wish she'd stayed home. When they got closer, she could hear what the men were saying.

"I told him I wasn't going to accept that thing for mailing." Kitty recognized the voice of the Postmaster.

"Who does he think he is anyway? A stranger coming in here and telling us how to think and what we should do with our own property." That was a voice Kitty didn't know.

An older voice spoke up. "James G. Birney is no stranger. Why, I remember when he was born, back in '92. Remember 'cause it was the year of statehood." The voice went on. "He went off for a while, and then he came back a couple of years ago. Reckon you moved here while he was gone."

"No matter." That was the second voice again. "He came back here then, a-freein' slaves and writin' papers tryin' to mess up men's minds and make 'em think Negroes are as good as us. Phooy!"

"Well, I'm not mailin' it out," the Postmaster said.

"Why don't he leave again?" A fourth voice spoke. "We don't need him here."

Kitty started to cry, and Gramps

picked her up. He didn't put her on his shoulders but held her against his chest. Just as he turned to start home, some men came out of the post office and she could see them over Gramps' shoulder.

"There's one of 'em," a man shouted. "That's old Mose Birney there carrying that Negro kid."

The men didn't come after them but Gramps ran all the way home anyway.

※ ※ ※ ※

They all stared sadly at each other. None of them could remember when black people were not treated exactly like white people. They had heard about it but somehow thinking of a real person like Mose and how it must have hurt him, and Kitty too, made it more real—and more sad.

But then David thought, *A real person? Was Mose a real person?* Strange that none of the others mentioned how weird it was that they all had him in their 'what ifs.'

"David, Mary Beth!" His mother's voice came from around the corner of the jail. A few seconds later she followed her voice and came into sight. "Come on, kids. The program is about to start."

They all trailed after her, looking sad and not talking at all. When they came to the stage area, they stopped. David glanced at his sister and friends and saw his own surprise mirrored on their faces. They'd all realized the same thing.

Seated around the stage were white people and black people and Asian people and Indian people and Hispanic people. And they were all laughing and joking together. Their 'what ifs' hadn't shown equality but it finally had come, not just to Kentucky but to the whole nation.

Then a woman stood up and asked everybody to join together in singing 'God Bless America.' Voices blended in the familiar song, and a funny little thrill warmed David's insides. Kentucky was part of America, the land of the free.

When the last notes of the song died away, a tall black man got up from a chair on the front row. The lady with the microphone smiled at him as he climbed the stairs to stand beside her on the stage. Then she turned her smile on the audience.

"Our speaker today is a man whose ancestors lived here in Danville during the era when Kentucky became a state. He has some fascinating stories to tell about that time period. Please join me in welcoming Mr. James Moses Birney."

David's mouth fell open. Slicker, Christy, and Mary Beth all turned shocked eyes toward him.

"How can that be?" Mary Beth asked, her voice nearly lost beneath the sound of the crowd's applause.

He shook his head. "I don't know." The hair on his arms stood straight up, and a feeling of excitement stirred his stomach. "But one thing's certain. We're free now. All the way through."

With a grin, he winked at his sister. It had taken some time for freedom to come to Kentucky, but there was a happy ending after all. They settled back in their chairs, eager to hear what James Moses Birney had to say.

Author's Notes

Adventure One

On July 9, 1984, on a site at the southern edge of the city of Danville, Kentucky, an archaeological team headed by Charles Niquette unearthed a partially finished spearhead.

In March and April of 1986, Niquette and his team, assisted by volunteers, both youth and adult, gathered enough information to determine that the site was periodically visited by early Kentuckians over a period of 10,000 years. It was used as a short-term camp by the Paleo Indian peoples (10,500 - 8,000 B.C.), the Archaic peoples (8,000 - 1,000 B.C.), and the Woodland peoples (1,000 B.C. - 900 A.D.).

Danville and the Boyle County area are rich in arrowheads, spearheads, and other artifacts which prove the existence of prehistoric peoples in the area.

Adventure Two

Bear Paw and Little Running Deer are fictional characters. But their village, way of life depicted here, and the legends they believed are historically accurate.

Cornstalk was a great Shawnee Chief who met his death at the fort at Point Pleasant. The details told here of him are true.

It is also true that the Shawnee originally inhabited the largest area of Kentucky than any other Indian tribe.

Bathsheba Lincoln did give birth to Abraham Lincoln's father, Thomas, in 1778, but there is nothing recorded to indicate that she was in the area of the Shawnee village in southern Ohio. Nevertheless, the Native American in our story spoke the truth when he said that his people have "contributed to this nation."

Adventure Three

Rebecca is a fictional girl but the lifestyle of her family written here is not.

Ann Kennedy Wilson Poague Lindsay McGinty outlived four husbands and did all the things mentioned here and much more. She was the first to take out a license to operate an Ordinary (or boarding house) in Kentucky. She was Ann Lindsay when the license was granted.

Jane Coomes began the first school in 'the west,' as Kentucky was known to be at the time. She also saved many lives by her knowledge of medicine. She left Harrodstown after ten years to move to Bardstown to be with others of her own faith.

Barney Stagner, known as the 'Old Dutchman,' was older when he brought his family to Fort Harrod and so his job, instead of something more physically demanding, was to guard the spring. Keeping it clean was necessary to the settlers, especially when the fort was under attack. Barney was not afraid of the Indians because, as he said, "I'm too old to hurt them." If he thought that meant they would not hurt him during his explorations through the woods, he was wrong. He was killed and the legend of his ghost guarding the spring is still told in Harrodsburg.

A reconstruction of Fort Harrod stands one block from the location of the original fort. In 1986, the Superintendent of Old Fort Harrod at that time, Susan Thompson

Barrington, very kindly opened the doors of the fort on a day it was closed to the public, and let me wander around to get the feel of the settlers. I'll never forget sitting in the schoolhouse on a hard bench and having Rebecca's story 'settle' in my mind. Colonel George Chinn, author of several books on Kentucky history, and Deputy Director of the Kentucky Historical Society at that time, granted me an interview. Both he and Susan Barrington answered many questions and told me about customs and stories that are not always found in books. A reconstruction of Fort Harrod stands one block from the location of the original fort.

Adventure Four

Mose, Kitty, Rachel, and Benji are all fictional characters, but the places and the events they saw in this book were very real.

Big and Little Harpe terrorized Kentuckians in the years 1798 and 1799. The three babies were born in the Danville jailhouse. The men escaped in March, 1799, leaving the women and children. Citizens of Danville put the women on trial and came to the conclusion that they were innocent victims. They took up food and money, and gave them a horse to help them get back to Tennessee. But the women took the things and joined their husbands in hiding. Big Harpe later killed Little Harpe's baby for crying too much. Together the men were responsible for at least 40 deaths of men, women, and children. Both men were eventually caught, tried, and executed.

"Father" David Rice, the Presbyterian minister, resigned from the tenth convention before it ended. That year he wrote an anti-slavery tract.

James Birney left Ireland in 1783 and settled in Danville, Kentucky in 1788 where he established a store. He and his wife Martha had a baby on February 4, 1792. They named him James Gillespie Birney. James G. left Danville for good in the fall of 1835 after his efforts to abolish slavery were rejected. He continued the fight against slavery for the rest of his life.

Discussion Questions

Adventure One

1. Do you think it would be fun to work on an archeological dig? What would you like about it? What would you dislike?
2. Would you like being an adventurer, or would it make you tired to travel all the time instead of having a settled place to live?
3. Do you know the word for the thing that Ke wanted? (Hint: The archeologist used it later when he told the children that the traveling tribes never had a permanent one.)
4. Do you enjoy reading about how people lived before modern times?
5. Can you think of something good about living in a time when there was no electricity, computers, television, or Internet?

Adventure Two

1. Have you ever gotten tired of somebody following you around?
2. Have you ever been lost? What did it feel like?
3. Why was Slicker afraid of Native Americans? Have you ever been afraid of someone who is different from you?
4. Bear Paw did not like white settlers. Why? Did he change his mind?
5. The old man Slicker met in the forest was proud of his Native American heritage. What reason does he give for that pride?

Adventure Three

1. Have you ever been separated from someone in your family, like Rebecca? Describe your feelings when you thought of that person.
2. How was school different in the fort in 1784 than it is today? Name as many ways as you can.
3. Were the first settlers of Kentucky brave or foolish? Describe why you think so.
4. Name one way the rules for the settlers in 1784 were different

from today.

5. What did both Rebecca and Christy discover was the most important thing?

Adventure Four

1. Some people find history boring, like Slicker, Mary Beth, and Christy did at first. Is it more interesting if you know more about the people who made history?

2. Was slavery an important issue when Kentucky became a state? What was the law made because some people were angry with those who wanted there to be no slavery in Kentucky? (It's not a law anymore.)

3. Early in Kentucky's history, females and people of other races were not allowed the same privileges as white men. Name some of the people in Adventure Four who were affected by that law. Aren't you glad it's not like that now?

4. At the end of the story when James Moses Birney stood up to speak, were you as surprised as David and the others?

Kentucky Adventures

1. Mary Beth, Slicker, Christy, and David learned a lot about Kentucky's past. Name a few things you learned while reading *Kentucky Adventures.*
2. Which adventure did you enjoy the most? Describe why.
3. If you could have your own "What If?" adventure, where and what year would you visit?

Acknowledgements

First of all and always my gratitude is to Virginia Smith who believes in my writing of all types. Thank you to Robert A. Powell who asked me to write some historical fiction for youth after he wrote Kentucky History curriculum for middle school students in the 1970 - 80's, and who also published the first form of the first adventure before giving it back to me. Thank you to Archeologist Charles Niquette, the head of the Danville archeological dig in 1986 who approved this first 'what if,' and to Susan Barrington and the Fort Harrod staff who let me in the Fort on a closed day to wander around and let 'what if's' flow into my mind for the third adventure. I'm so grateful to the late Colonel George Chinn, author of several books on Kentucky and former Deputy Director of the Kentucky Historical Society, for answering many questions and telling me customs and stories that are not always found in books. Thank you to Malinda Raines for the wonderful illustrations.

Books by Amy Barkman

Fiction for Young People
Kentucky Adventures
Which Witch?

Fiction for Adults
Murder at Tapestry Court
To Love Again

Nonfiction for Adults
Everyday Spiritual Warfare